SEAL

illustrated by Lynne Cherry

E. P. DUTTON • NEW YORK

Big seals, little seals.
Look at all the seals.

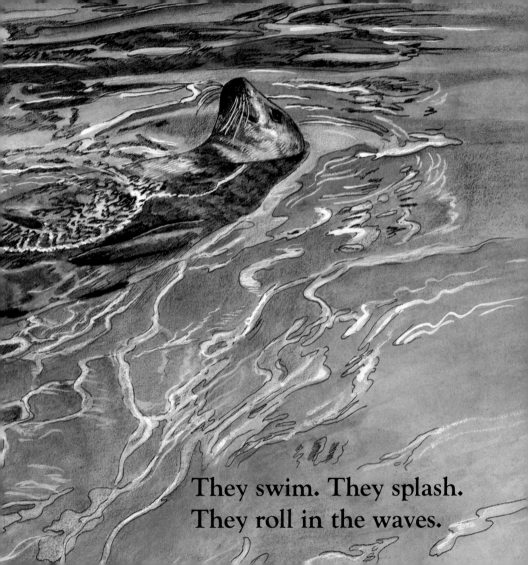

They swim. They splash.
They roll in the waves.

They dive

deep

deep

down

and then come up again to breathe.

The water is cold,
but not to a seal.
It has a sleek fur coat
to keep it warm.

A seal's home is by the sea.

for Gunvor, Steve, Synne and Kari-Anna Wing,
my good friends whose home is by the sea

Text copyright © 1987 by E. P. Dutton
Illustrations copyright © 1987 by Lynne Cherry

All rights reserved.
Licensed by World Wildlife Fund®

Published in the United States by E. P. Dutton,
2 Park Avenue, New York, N.Y. 10016

Published simultaneously in Canada by
Fitzhenry & Whiteside Limited, Toronto

Text and editing: Lucia Monfried   Designer: Isabel Warren-Lynch

Printed in Singapore by Tien Wah Press
First Edition   CUSA & P   10 9 8 7 6 5 4 3 2 1

Library of Congress Cataloging-in-Publication Data

Cherry, Lynne.
  Seal.

  (Help save us books)
  Summary: A look at seals as they swim and dive in
the sea.

  1. Seals (Animals)—Pictorial works—Juvenile
literature.   [1. Seals (Animals)]   I. Monfried, Lucia.
II. Title.   III. Series.
QL737.P6C47   1987   599.74'8   86-24030
ISBN 0-525-44304-5